THE DRAGONSITTER:
Trick or Treat?

Josh Lacey

Illustrated by Garry Parsons

LITTLE, BROWN AND COMPANY
New York • Boston

Text copyright © 2016 by Josh Lacey
Illustrations copyright © 2016 by Garry Parsons

Cover design by Angela Taldone. Cover art © 2016 by Garry Parsons.
Cover hand-lettering © 2015 by David Coulson

Little, Brown and Company
Hachette Book Group
1290 Avenue of the Americas, New York, NY 10104
Visit us at lb-kids.com

Originally published in 2017 by Andersen Press Limited in Great Britain
First U.S. Edition: July 2017

Little, Brown and Company is a division of Hachette Book Group, Inc.
The Little, Brown name and logo are trademarks of Hachette Book Group, Inc.

The publisher is not responsible for websites (or their content)
that are not owned by the publisher.

Library of Congress Cataloging-in-Publication Data 2017930065

ISBNs: 978-0-316-55582-1 (hardcover), 978-0-316-55584-5 (pbk.),
978-0-316-55580-7 (ebook)

Printed in the United States of America

LSC-C

10 9 8 7 6 5 4 3 2

THE DRAGONSITTER:
Trick or Treat?

From: Edward Smith-Pickle

To: Morton Pickle

Date: Tuesday, October 24

Subject: Halloween

Attachments: Ghost and monster

Dear Uncle Morton,

Can I borrow your dragons?

Next week there is a costume competition at the Halloween Parade.

The first-place prize is a new computer, which is exactly what we need.

Our computer is Dad's old one. He left it behind when he moved out, and that was four years ago. It was already ancient then.

Also, Emily spilled a glass of milk on the keyboard and now the keys only work if you press them really hard.

All our problems would be solved if we won that prize.

Unfortunately, we don't have very good costumes.

I was planning to go as Frankenstein's monster, but I can't find any bolts for my neck.

Emily wants to be a ghost, but that just means wearing a sheet and going "Whoooo, whoooo" and she's never going to win anything for that.

Could we borrow your dragons?

With them we'd be sure to win first place.

We would only actually need Ziggy and Arthur for one night, but Mom says you are welcome to stay for the whole week, as long as you don't mind sleeping on the sofa.

Granny is staying for fall break, and I bet she would really like to see you, too.

Love from your favorite nephew,

Eddie

From: Morton Pickle

To: Edward Smith–Pickle

Date: Wednesday, October 25

Subject: Re: Halloween

Attachments: I ❤ Oregon

Dear Eddie,

I would have loved to join you for Halloween.
There are few things that I like more than tricks
and treats. Sadly, though, I must stay here in
Scotland because I am hard at work preparing
for my trip to Oregon in search of Bigfoot.

However, Gordon has kindly volunteered
to come in my place. I think he just wants
an excuse to see your mother. He is always
complaining about how much he misses her.

As you will see for yourself, Arthur is going
through a growth spurt at the moment and

hasn't quite mastered the art of breathing fire. You may want to keep an extinguisher handy.

Thank you for the picture of your costumes. You both look lovely, but I can see why you need a little help. I'm sure the dragons will be just the ticket. If they aren't, perhaps you could persuade your mother to buy you a new computer? Or a second-hand one? Surely they aren't too expensive these days.

What a pity that I will not get to see my own mother. But please do send Granny my best wishes.

With love from your affectionate uncle,

Morton

Dear Uncle Morton,

Thank you very much for sending the dragons with Gordon.

I promise we will take very good care of them.

I know we've had a few disasters before, but this time will be different.

I just hope we win first place. The computer isn't going to live much longer. It keeps moaning and groaning, and the screen has gone wobbly.

I asked Mom if she could buy us a new one, but she said single-parent families can't afford luxuries like brand-new computers.

She said even a second-hand one would be too much for us in the current economic climate.

I asked what the current economic climate was, and she said gloomy.

Love,

Eddie

Dear Uncle Morton,

Do you like our tam-o'-shanters?

Gordon gave them to me and Emily. He says we look like proper wee Scots.

He also brought lots of presents for Mom. We just ate some of the smoked salmon with our scrambled eggs.

Mom said it was the most delicious breakfast of her entire life, and I think it might have been mine, too.

I see what you mean about Arthur breathing

fire. He's already had a few accidents. But Mom said it didn't matter.

I think she's just happy to see Gordon.

Also, he peed on the carpet. (Arthur, I mean, not Gordon.) But you can't blame him for that. He must have been desperate after driving all the way from Scotland.

When everyone has recovered, we're going to make our costumes.

I've changed my mind about Frankenstein's monster. I'm going to be an Egyptian mummy instead.

Emily is still planning to go as a ghost, and the dragons can just be themselves.

I'll send you lots of pictures.

Love,

Eddie

From: Edward Smith-Pickle

To: Morton Pickle

Date: Saturday, October 28

Subject: HELP!!!!!!!!

📎 **Attachments:** The proposal

Dear Uncle Morton,

We have a big problem, and we need your help.

This afternoon, Gordon asked Mom to marry him.

Obviously that's not the problem. We all really like Gordon. Especially Mom.

The problem is he got down on one knee and pulled a ring from his pocket.

Then he said, "Will you marry me?"

Mom literally couldn't speak.

If only she had said "yes" right away.

12

Then Gordon could have put the ring on her finger and everything would have been fine.

Unfortunately, Mom just stood there with her mouth open, staring at the ring as if she'd never seen anything like it before.

Which gave Arthur enough time to fly across the room and snatch it out of Gordon's hand.

I don't know why he did that. I've never eaten a ring myself, but I can't imagine it's very tasty.

Even so, he swallowed it quicker than you could say "I do".

Mom and Gordon tried to force Arthur's mouth open and pull the ring right out again, which wasn't exactly smart.

Gordon is very upset. Not just about his burned fingers, but also about the ring.

It belonged to his great-aunt Isla. She wore it every day for sixty-seven years.

Now it's inside Arthur's tummy, and we don't know how to get it out.

Do you have any brilliant ideas?

Love,

Eddie

14

From: Morton Pickle

To: Edward Smith-Pickle

Date: Saturday, October 28

Subject: Re: HELP!!!!!!!!

📎 **Attachments:** A wee dram

Dear Eddie,

I'm terribly sorry to hear about Gordon's great-aunt's ring.

Unfortunately, I can't imagine any way to extract it from Arthur's stomachs. (As you will remember from reading my book, dragons have three.)

If I were you, I would simply keep Arthur indoors for the next couple of days. The ring is sure to progress steadily through his guts and emerge eventually in his poop. Make sure you check them thoroughly. Once you have washed the ring, it will be as good as new, if not even better.

15

To speed up the process, you could feed him some dried fruit. Figs or apricots would be perfect.

Don't forget to keep all your doors and windows firmly closed. All would be lost if Arthur was allowed to leave the house and take flight. You would never find the ring again if he pooped in midair.

On a quite different subject, please share my congratulations with Gordon and your mother.

I hope they don't mind, but I have already announced the good news to Gordon's uncle, Mr. McDougall. Tonight we had a drink together in celebration.

Is Gordon planning to move south? Or are you all going to come and live in Scotland? I hope you do. I couldn't imagine having nicer neighbors than you and Emily.

With love from your affectionate uncle,

Morton

From: Edward Smith-Pickle

To: Morton Pickle

Date: Saturday, October 28

Subject: The oven

Attachments: Potatoes

Dear Uncle Morton,

I asked Mom if we were moving to Scotland or staying here, and she said she hasn't had a moment to think about the wedding, let alone where we're going to live.

Mostly she's been worrying about how to get the ring out of Arthur.

She said she was going to kill him. I am almost sure she was joking. Even so, I locked him in the oven.

He didn't seem to mind. He just curled up and went to sleep.

I think he must have known it was for his own
safety.

I would have liked to keep him in there until he pooped, but we're having baked potatoes with dinner.

Mom said turning the oven on would be fine, Arthur or no Arthur, but Gordon wasn't sure that was such a good idea.

I don't think he was too concerned about Arthur's personal safety. He just thought Arthur might explode, taking the ring with him.

So now he's in a cardboard box on the kitchen floor.

Love,

Eddie

Dear Uncle Morton,

Mom says we can't go to the Halloween Parade unless we get the ring out of Arthur.

I asked why not, and she said we have to understand that actions have consequences.

I said that's not fair because it wasn't me and Emily who swallowed the ring, but she said that's not the point.

I asked what was the point, and she said I should think about it.

I have been thinking about it. A lot. But I still don't know.

All I do know is this: if we are going to win that new computer, we have to get the ring out of Arthur.

Do you have any other ideas apart from apricots and figs?

I've been feeding him both, but they don't seem to be having any effect.

He just won't poop.

What can we do, Uncle Morton?

We need that computer. We really do.

The screen on this one is flickering so much it's given me a headache.

Also, the space bar fell off. I strapped it back on with Scotch tape, but I don't know how much longer it will last.

Love,

Eddie

Dear Uncle Morton,

Today Arthur ate a package of apricots and a package of figs plus six sausages and two lamb chops, but nothing came out the other end.

Granny said cod liver oil would get things moving.

We had some in the bathroom cabinet, so I tried to give a teaspoon to Arthur, but he wouldn't touch it.

Granny says hello, by the way. She arrived from Spain this morning.

She wants to know why you never go and visit her.

I said you were very busy with Bigfoot and the yeti and your dragons, and she asked what kind of son is too busy to visit his own mother, Bigfeet or no Bigfeet.

Also, she wants to know when you're going to settle down and have some children of your own.

She thinks you should take a leaf out of Mom's book.

I told her you have the dragons instead, but she said they don't count.

Love,

Eddie

Dear Uncle Morton,

The costume competition is tomorrow night. Our costumes are finished. Mine looks awesome, and so does Emily's. I bet we'd win first place.

But Arthur still hasn't pooped, so we're not even going.

I can't understand why he won't. I've fed him about a hundred figs and apricots. Also, he had three candy apples.

Mom spent the afternoon making them. She said she needed something to take her mind off the ring.

I only ate half of mine. It wasn't very good. But Arthur gulped down three of them without even blinking.

Granny said we should hold him upside down and shake him till the ring comes out.

I explained about Arthur's new fire-breathing abilities, and Granny said she wasn't scared of a few flames.

I said, even so, it probably wasn't a good idea, but she did not care.

I really don't know why Granny got so mad about her new shoes. If you fed me two packages of figs and three candy apples, then held me upside down and shook me, I would probably be sick, too.

Granny says if you had a scrap of decency you would come down here yourself and clear up this whole mess.

I don't know whether she means the barf or the swallowed ring.

Maybe she means both.

But do you think you could do that, Uncle Morton? Couldn't you just come here and sort things out?

We really do need some help.

Eddie

From: Morton Pickle

To: Edward Smith-Pickle

Date: Monday, October 30

Subject: Re: Candy apples

Dear Eddie,

I'm terribly sorry, but I simply don't have time to come and help you. You wouldn't believe how many books have been written about Bigfoot, and I am hoping to read them all before I leave.

At the same time, I am cleaning and checking every inch of my camping equipment. Yesterday I found a big hole burned through the middle of my tent. Arthur must have had another accident while I wasn't looking. I spent the entire evening sewing it up with a square of new canvas and some thick thread.

I am terribly sorry that he is proving to be so obstinate. I can only suggest that you try massaging his stomachs. Perhaps you can ease things toward the exit.

I hope the ring emerges in time for the competition and you manage to win first place. I shall be thinking of you tomorrow night.

What a pity that I shall not get to see my mother. Please send her my best wishes. I shall make every effort to visit her in Spain as soon as I can.

With love from your affectionate uncle,

Morton

From: Edward Smith–Pickle

To: Morton Pickle

Date: Tuesday, October 31

Subject: Costume changes

Attachments: Mummy; Devil; Witch

Dear Uncle Morton,

I wish I could say Happy Halloween, but it's really not.

There are only a few hours until the start of the costume competition, but Arthur still hasn't pooped.

I don't know why we even bothered trying on our costumes.

I did what you suggested and massaged his tummy, but he didn't like that one bit. In fact, he blew a big blast of fire directly at me.

Gordon says my Egyptian mummy costume looks even more authentic with a bit of smoke damage, but I know he's just trying to be nice.

Luckily, I've got a skeleton costume upstairs in my closet, so I'm going to change into that.

Gordon's costume is amazing. I never would have thought he could look like the devil, but he

really does. He even has horns on his head and a forked tail that swings from side to side when he walks.

Granny looks quite frightening, too, although she's just wearing a witch's hat made from a cereal box.

Even Emily is a bit scary in her sheet.

It's a pity no one is going to see us dressed up.

Eddie

From: Edward Smith-Pickle

To: Morton Pickle

Date: Tuesday, October 31

Subject: Zombie attack

 Attachments: More candy apples; Zombie rampage

Dear Uncle Morton,

The costume competition starts in one hour, but we're still at home.

Gordon suggested we try apple bobbing. Apparently that's a tradition in Scotland on Halloween.

But I don't feel like bobbing for apples.

I want to win first place in the costume competition.

By the way, your dragons haven't just ruined Halloween for us. They've now messed it up for several other people, too, because only ten

minutes ago, the doorbell rang. I grabbed the tray of candy apples and opened the front door.

There were three zombies outside waving their arms and shouting, "Trick or treat! Trick or treat!"

They were dripping blood all over the front yard.

They looked very realistic.

In fact, Ziggy must have thought they were
actually zombies because she shoved me aside

and breathed a great gust of orange fire at them.

Then she chased them down the front path.

I've never seen zombies run so fast.

If Ziggy carries on like this, we're going to have a lot of candy apples left over.

Eddie

From: Edward Smith-Pickle

To: Morton Pickle

Date: Tuesday, October 31

Subject: Trick or treat?

 Attachments: Neighbors; Parade; Sugar rush; Fireworks

Dear Uncle Morton,

Happy Halloween!

This time I really mean it.

Mom let us go to the Halloween Parade.

Gordon persuaded her to change her mind.
I don't know how he did it, but they were
whispering for ages, and then she said yes.

I think she must be in a good mood because of
getting married.

Granny said let's see if it lasts.

I asked if she meant the good mood or the marriage, and Granny said, "Either would be nice."

Anyway, Mom said we could go trick-or-treating and enter the costume competition as long as we behaved ourselves, and didn't talk to strangers, and looked both ways before crossing the road, and always did exactly what Granny and Gordon said.

Mom stayed behind with Arthur, just in case he pooped, so only five of us went: Emily the ghost, Granny the witch, Gordon the devil, me the skeleton, and Ziggy as herself.

First we went trick-or-treating.

Gordon let us ring the bell of any house with a pumpkin in the window.

You wouldn't believe how much candy we got.

Every house was just the same. We hardly even got a chance to say "Trick or treat!" People took one look at Ziggy and handed over whatever they had.

Gordon said we had enough candy to open a candy store.

I know you don't like Ziggy having too many sweets, so I only gave her a few.

Even so, she got a bit of a sugar rush. Her eyes went a bit wild and her whiskers started twitching.

I didn't give her any more after that, but
unfortunately Emily handed over a bunch
of lollipops and two whole packs of gummy
bears.

Ziggy gulped them down without even bothering
to take off the wrappers.

Then we went downtown for the Halloween
Parade and the costume competition.

The street was jam-packed with ghosts and
ghouls and vampires and witches and wizards

and trolls and goblins, plus two Batmans, three Robins, and a princess.

We all marched past the judges. They were taking notes on all the costumes and whispering to one another.

What happened next was probably my fault.

I was trying to look really skeletony in front of the judges, so I wasn't paying very much attention to Ziggy.

I don't know if I could have done anything even if I had been watching her, but at least I could have tried.

The first thing I heard was a loud hiccup.

Then she gave an enormous burp.

When I turned to look at her, she was flapping her wings.

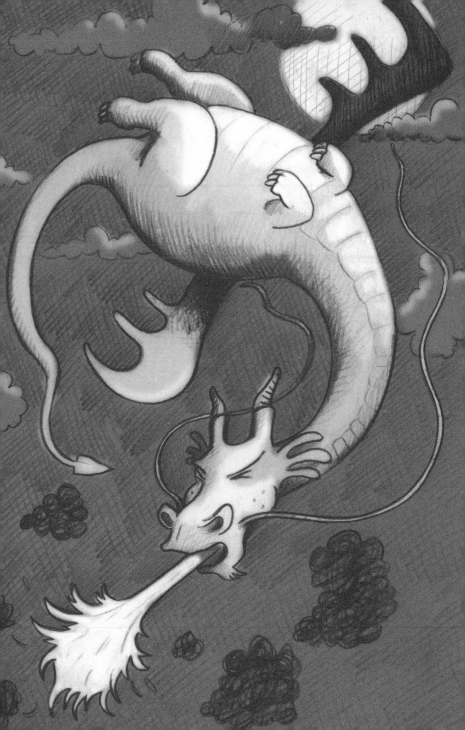

I tried to grab her, but it was already too late.

She flew straight up into the air and did a somersault.

Then she did about seventeen more while breathing fire in every direction.

Everyone was cheering and clapping.

It was like our own personal fireworks display.

The judges were watching her, too. They were all pointing into the sky and looking completely amazed. I hope they didn't forget to look at our costumes.

I wanted to go back and walk in front of them a second time, but Granny said it was time to go home.

She's used to the weather in Spain, so she feels the cold more than the rest of us. She says it gets into her bones.

I hope you're having a good Halloween in Scotland. Did you get any trick-or-treaters on your island?

Love,

Eddie

Dear Uncle Morton,

I hope you can read this, because there is a fizzing sound coming from the back of the computer and I don't know how much longer it will even work.

Also, the space bar fell off again and now I'm using half a pencil instead.

Gordon says I get full marks for ingenuity, but first–place prize in the costume competition would be even better. I just hope the judges got a proper look at our costumes.

They are announcing the prizes tomorrow, so we are all keeping our fingers crossed.

Arthur still hasn't pooped. His tummy is getting so big he can hardly even fly anymore. I'm really quite worried about what will happen if he doesn't poop soon.

Do you think dragons can explode?

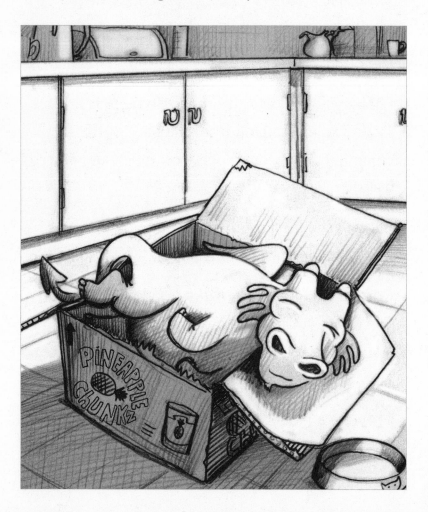

Mom says he has to stay in his cardboard box just in case.

She doesn't want bits of him all over her kitchen.

You will be glad to hear that Ziggy is fine after her sugar rush. She has spent the whole day asleep.

We haven't given her any more candy.

We haven't actually had any more ourselves. Mom confiscated the whole pile and put them in the cabinet.

We're going to be allowed one a day on weekdays and two on Saturdays and Sundays.

At that rate, they'll last us until next Christmas.

Love,

Eddie

Dear Uncle Morton,

We didn't win the competition.

We did get a prize, but it wasn't first.

Gordon says third prize is just as good as first, but I know he's only trying to be nice.

Also, a bunch of flowers really isn't as good as a new computer.

Mom says we'll have to wait until she gets a pay raise.

I just hope she gets one soon. The noises coming out of this computer are getting stranger all the time.

Also, you owe me some candy.

Actually Ziggy and Arthur do, but Mom says you're their owner, so any thefts or damages are your responsibility.

This morning before anyone came down for breakfast your dragons broke into the cabinet.

I don't know how they got in there. The latch on the door is too hard for me to open. But somehow they managed to twist it around.

They took all my candy, and all of Emily's, too, and some others that Mom was keeping for a special occasion.

To be honest, we're quite annoyed with them.

I wouldn't have minded giving them a few of my candies, but why did they have to eat them all?

Granny says you were always stealing sweets from the cupboard when you were a little boy.

I couldn't imagine you stealing anything from anywhere, but Granny said you used to be a little terror.

Were you really, Uncle Morton?

Love,

Eddie

P.S. Click this link to see the whole story: **http//www.bestlocalnews.com/vampire-wins-first-prize.html**

COUNTY NEWS UPDATE:
Vampire Wins First Prize in Halloween Parade

WEDNESDAY, NOVEMBER 1st   **PLACE AN AD**   **SUBSCRIBE**

This year more than two hundred people attended the traditional Halloween Parade.

During the evening, they were lucky enough to see a surprise firework display provided by a local resident.

The costume competition was judged by a panel of local experts, who said the standard was higher than ever.

After a long and heated discussion, the judges awarded first prize to a vampire.

Agnes Kranowski, 11, was dressed as the daughter of Count Dracula, while her brother Tomas went as her coffin.

Agnes and Tomas went home with a brand-new laptop from the Technology Store, the perfect place to upgrade your computer and purchase any accessories.

Second prize of $50 of books from The Village Bookstore went to Michelle Hussein, 7, who was dressed as a headless ghost.

Third Prize of $10 of flowers from Betty's Blooms went to a skeleton and his magnificent Chinese dragon kite.

The winner of the third prize has not yet come forward to claim their flowers. If you are the owner of the skeleton costume and the kite, please contact Betty at Betty's Blooms.

Dear Uncle Morton,

Arthur has pooped out the ring!

It must have been the sugar that did it.

When we came down for breakfast there was an enormous piece of steaming black poop on the carpet near the back door.

On top of the poop was the ring.

It looked like the cherry on a cake.

Unfortunately it isn't really a ring anymore. It's more like a lump.

The gold must have melted while it was inside Arthur.

The diamond is fine. It came unstuck from the rest of the ring, but it's perfectly clean now that we've washed off all the poop.

Unfortunately, Mom can't wear the diamond on her finger without its ring.

Gordon is very upset. He says his great-aunt Isla would be turning in her grave if she could see it.

Emily said rings don't really matter and what's important is getting married to the person you love.

Gordon said his great-aunt Isla wouldn't think so.

I hope he isn't having second thoughts.

Love,

Eddie

Dear Uncle Morton,

I am writing this on OUR NEW COMPUTER!

Can you tell?

It's amazing being able to see the screen.

Also, all the keys on the keyboard work. Even the space bar.

Gordon bought it for us.

Actually, he didn't really buy it for *us*. He bought it for Mom, so she can do her spreadsheets for the wedding.

But Mom says Emily and I can use it whenever

we want, as long as we're not playing games or wasting time.

We got it this afternoon from the Technology Store. While we were there I saw the computer

which was first prize in the costume competition. It looked quite nice, but ours is even better.

After the computer shop we went to Betty's Blooms to collect our prize.

Betty wanted to know why we hadn't brought our kite to the shop. I explained she was asleep.

She wanted to know where she could get one of her own, and I said she would have to find the right cave in Outer Mongolia.

Also, she wrote down the name of your book. She's going to get it out of the library.

Then Betty gave us the $10 gift certificate, and we bought a big bunch of flowers.

They were really pretty.

In fact, Gordon thought they were so pretty he bought them from us for $20.

I said that was much too much, but he said it was money well spent.

He gave $10 to me and $10 to Emily and the flowers to Mom.

I've got to go now. Mom and Gordon want to use the new computer to plan their wedding.

We've been helping them decide the menu.

They're going to have a ceilidh.

I thought that was something to eat, but actually it's a kind of Scottish dance. And it's pronounced "kay-lee," if you were wondering.

Gordon has been teaching us how to do it.

Love,

Eddie

P.S. Mom asks if would you be able to give her away?

From: Morton Pickle

To: Edward Smith-Pickle

Date: Saturday, November 4

Subject: Re: Computer

Dear Eddie,

Congratulations on your new computer!

I'm terribly sorry that Arthur ate all your candy. Of course I shall buy you and Emily more when we next meet.

I certainly didn't steal any sweets myself when I was a boy. My mother must have mixed me up with someone else.

Please tell your own mother that I would be flattered to give her away at her wedding. When will it be? I shall put the date in my diary and make sure that I am in the country.

You will be glad to hear that my preparations

for Oregon have gone swimmingly, and I shall be setting out on the trail of Bigfoot just before Christmas. Would you like to come, too?

With love from your affectionate uncle,

Morton

Dear Uncle Morton,

I hope you're going to be at home today, because Ziggy and Arthur are on their way back to Scotland.

Gordon left first thing this morning. If he doesn't hit any bad traffic, they should be back in time for dinner.

Mom is still feeling a bit weepy.

They haven't decided the date of the wedding, but Mom says you will be the first to know.

I asked shouldn't me and Emily be the first to know, and Mom said it was just an expression. So maybe you will be the third to know.

I'd better go now. We're taking Granny to the airport. She's flying back to Spain.

She is very sorry she didn't get to see you, but at least she met your dragons.

Love,

Eddie

P.S. I asked Mom if I could go to Oregon with you to search for Bigfoot, and she said only when I'm 18. Could you wait until then?

THE DRAGONSITTER Series

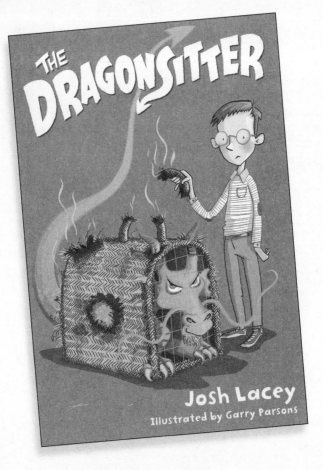

THE DRAGONSITTER

Josh Lacey

Illustrated by Garry Parsons

COLLECT THEM ALL!

If you enjoyed

THE DRAGONSITTER: Trick or Treat?,

you might also like these series,

available now!

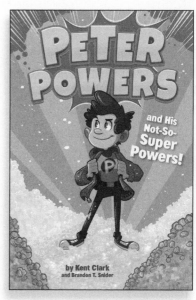

 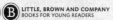

About the Author

JOSH LACEY is the author of many books for children, including *The Island of Thieves*, *Bearkeeper*, and the Grk series. He worked as a journalist, a teacher, and a screenwriter before writing his first book, *A Dog Called Grk*. Josh lives in London with his wife and daughters.

About the Illustrator

GARRY PARSONS has illustrated several books for children and is the author and illustrator of *Krong!*, winner of the Perth and Kinross Picture Book Award. Garry lives in London.